C000155044

Birth of the Wicked

Ashley Bríon

Published by Ashley Bríon, 2022.

BIRTH OF THE WICKED

First edition. May 31, 2022.

Written by Ashley Bríon.

Also by Ashley Bríon

Brooke de Láuront
The Black Rogue
Secrets in Paris
Letters From Home

Standalone
Caged With A Rebel
Birth of the Wicked
Illusion at Midnight
The Christmas Post

Watch for more at https://www.slucas0.wixsite.com/authorash-leybrion.

Dedicated to all the women (and you too men), who were bullied until the point of no return. You are loved, and you matter.

1: Merry ye meet

Valerie was late for class... again. She forgot to plug in her phone the night before and of course it died in the middle of the night. She was hyperventilating as she gathered her books in her backpack, grabbed the first dress she saw in the closet, slipped on her sandals, and high-tailed it through her dorm. Luckily, her class was only the next building over, past the thru-road and commuter parking lot, so she didn't have too far to go. As she ran out the dorm's front doors, the chilly October rain poured, making the air crisp and cool instead of muggy and hot like it had been the past few days.

Ugh, she thought, *way to go, stupid, you didn't grab an umbrella.* As soon as she went to make a run for it, a truck passed in front of her, swerving to hit the giant puddle next to the sidewalk. Water-soaked Valerie like a dog after jumping in the river. Her clothes and backpack were dripping wet, and her hair was clinging to her face. As she looked toward the truck, she could hear Luke Bryan blaring from the radio and men laughing like the sound of a strangled pig.

"Hey, Val! Try getting bigger glasses so you can see a truck coming toward you! Or can't you see over those buck teeth of yours, you Princess Bride reject!" The man said as he got out of his Ford F-250. He hopped out of the truck. He wore a red and black plaid shirt, tight jeans, and cowboy boots.

1

Valerie could feel the heat rising in her face, but no one could see her tears over the rain. She ran as fast as she could past them, through the pouring rain and up the macadam walkway on the hill toward the entrance to the Humanities building. When she reached the door to her classroom, she could see her best friend sitting near the door taking notes, just as Professor Brig was writing on the whiteboard giving the lecture. Valerie quickly opened the door and tried to sneak to her seat, but the sound of her squeaking shoes squishing across the floor and the loud click of the door made the entire class turn towards her.

"Miss Bennet, would you like to enlighten the class to your tardiness... again?" Professor Brig said. He didn't even bother looking up from the whiteboard as he addressed her.

"I'm sorry, Professor Brig, I forgot to charge my phone, so my alarm didn't go off this morning," Valerie said sheepishly still standing by the door. Her best friend Cordelia let out a sigh and put her head on the desk in defeat.

"Take your seat, Miss Bennet. And next time, remember to dry your clothes before you take them out of the washer."

Valerie dripped her way over to her seat next to Cordelia. Professor Brig continued to give his lecture on the Medici family as Cordelia flicked Valerie in the arm.

"What the hell?" Cordelia mumbled under her breath. "Why are you dripping wet and why didn't you charge your phone? You really need an actual alarm clock."

"Cole drove by, and I fell asleep studying and forgot. Does that sum it up for you?" Valerie mumbled back.

"Fuckin' Cole...you can copy my notes after class."

"Miss Chamberlain, do you wish to speak to the class, or can I keep teaching?" Professor Brig said right next to Cordelia, making them nearly jump out of their skin.

"Oh, no, Professor Brig, I was just telling Val she could copy my notes after class," she said smoothly.

Professor Brig turned up his nose and strode back toward the front of the classroom. "Maybe if Miss Bennet would get a proper alarm, she would be here on time for her notes. Leave the gossip until after class and pay attention."

Stupid   tweed-jacket-wearing-bald-headed-Gary-Busey-lookin'-fuck, Valerie thought as she pulled her notebook out of her soggy backpack. Luckily, her textbooks and notebooks didn't get wet, so she could continue to take notes for the rest of class.

Forty-five minutes later, she was semi-dry and the torturous class from hell was over. Valerie left so quickly Cordelia almost tripped over her own shoes trying to keep up with her. As soon as they quickly walked through the halls, through the door, and out into the courtyard by the fountain, Cordelia finally spoke up.

"Okay, what the fuck was that back there? You come into class late, soaking wet, and then because you get berated by the biggest asshole professor in our major that, by the way, *nobody* else likes either, you take off like you drank milky booze on a hot day? C'mon, cough up. What's the deets?"

Valerie sighed as she sat on the bench near the fountain.

"I'm tired, Cor. I've been a fuck up all my life and now I can barely get college right. We're only halfway into the semester and I've been late three times to his class and a few others. People push me, act like I'm invisible, tease me, and treat me like shit. It's like bad luck follows me everywhere! Today I wake up late with a dead phone, didn't have any clean clothes because I forgot I needed to go to the other washer in Demeester Hall. Then I come out here to see it's pouring down rain, and Cole decides to purposely splash me with his truck and call me a Princess Bride reject with my big glasses and buck teeth. I don't have buck teeth! They're just a little off from not getting braces as a kid is all. Just... why me? Why does everyone hate me?" Valerie broke down into tears.

"Hey..." Cor said as she sat down and hugged her, "It's ok. Honestly, fuck them. Cole especially. He's not worth it and he'll never be worth it. He's just mad because he'll never get a girl like you and has a limp tiny ass dick. Thing probably can't even rate on a centimeter ruler. Ok, so yeah, you might seem to have some bad luck all the time, maybe we just need to get you some good juju stuff. Like a lucky rabbit foot or one of those bobble things you put on your car dash."

"Cor... that's a bobblehead, not a good luck charm. You're thinking of the angels people put in their car visor."

"Yeah, those things. But everything's gonna be fine. I mean, look. You got into college on a full ride because you were like the smartest person in school. You were always very coordinated when it came to marching band and figuring out instructions. You have me. And you know I'm not gonna let anything bad happen to you. These are all minor things. One day all this petty shit will go away, and you'll look back and laugh from your fancy penthouse in London or some other awesome exotic place across the sea. Trust me. Just don't let these bullies get you down. It'll eat you up and start to rot you from inside you if you don't."

"Yeah, I know. Sometimes I just don't know what to do. Thanks, Cor." Valerie sunk into the bench, back arched with her head over the back, and looked at Cordelia.

"Anytime," Cordelia said, patting her on the back. "Now can we go get lunch? I'm starving. I need a pizza in my life."

Valerie laughed. "You always need pizza in your life."

"And what's wrong with that?" Cordelia said with her hand on her hip and a sassy tone.

AT THE PIZZA SHOP UP the street from the campus, Valerie and Cordelia munched on a pepperoni pizza as they chatted about class and went over notes Valerie missed.

"So, the Medici family was, like, huge thanks to Cosimo with all the banking going on... hey, are you listening?" Cordelia said.

Valerie *was* listening until two women walked into the shop. She couldn't help but stare at them, while a feeling she couldn't explain unfurled in her belly. It was a mixture of awe, fear, and curiosity. There was something about them in their black lace dresses, high black pumps, chainmail necklaces with crystals dangling from them, and chunky silver bracelets with pentacles on them that had her mesmerized; drawn to them.

"Huh? Yeah, yeah. Medici... banking family..." Valerie trailed off as she continued to watch the two women.

Cordelia turned to see what Valerie was staring at and turned white.

"Val! *Stop looking at them.* They'll curse you or turn you into a frog or something!"

Valerie looked at Cordelia incredulously. "Huh? The fuck is you going on about? It's just two women eating some subs."

"They're not just *any* women, Val. Everybody on campus knows they're part of a cult. One of them witch covens, ya know?"

"Witches, huh? Just because they're part of a coven doesn't automatically make it a cult. Now the KKK? *That's* a cult," Valerie said, shaking her Pepsi cup toward Cordelia and taking a sip.

"You don't wanna fuck with them, Val. They're bad news. Rumors around campus say they killed a boy," Cordelia began to whisper closer to Valerie across the table. "They never found his body."

"I know Halloween is like a month and a half away, but that doesn't mean it's ok to start spooky rumors about people, Cor."

"It wasn't me!" Cordelia squealed, placing her hands on her chest. "I just heard it from Kelly who heard it from Jake, and he heard it from DeAndre, and he heard it..."

"Ok, ok! I get your point. Look, they're probably misunderstood, just like me. And you're friends with me. Maybe they just need some friends." Valerie shrugged.

Cordelia snorted as she took another bite of a mozzarella stick. "Yeah, sure. Friends. They probably use them as sacrifices to their ancient gods."

Valerie rolled her eyes. Sometimes Cordelia could be impressionable and believe anything anyone says.

"Well," Cordelia started to stuff her face with pizza, "Vere gonna be wate to cass iv we don' 'urry."

Valerie raised an eyebrow. "I'm sorry, was that English?"

Cordelia swallowed her massive bites of pizza. "C'mon, we gotta go! Take the pizza and let's hurry or we'll be late to Astronomy lab."

"You go ahead, I'll pay and catch up," Valerie waved her away absently.

It was Cordelia's turn to raise an eyebrow. "Excuse me?"

"No, seriously. Save my seat."

Cordelia stood, but quickly sat back down, wagging a finger at Valerie. "Don't. Talk. To. Them. I mean it. You don't want to be friends with them."

"Ok, ok. I won't talk to them," Valerie said as Cordelia walked by her, gave her a hug, and walked out the door, the bell above the door tinkling as it closed behind her.

Valerie did her best to ignore the two women and stop staring at them, but as soon as she went to inch herself out of the booth to grab a pizza box, she was pushed back in, and she heard two voices speaking to her.

"Hey."

"Hi."

Oh no...instantly the two women were in her booth and talking to her.

"Hi, um..." Valerie stuttered, "I'm sorry but I really have to go I'm late for class..."

"What's your hurry, honey?" said the woman with long black hair and heavily kohl-ringed eyes. Her skin was a mix between tan and pale, like she only saw the sun a few days a year.

"We don't mean any harm. We just want to talk. Is that ok?" the other woman said. She had shoulder-length, green, curly hair, and eyes as green as a vine snake.

Both women were incredibly beautiful. They had soft curves, full breasts accented by their tight black and red corsets with metal latches covered in lace overtop of their long bell-sleeve lace dresses. The black-haired woman wore a short dress, and the green-haired woman wore a long gown-length dress that sparkled in the light. Their skin looked smooth and soft, their lips plump under a dark void of black and blood red lipstick, and their faces didn't have a single blemish.

"I don't have anything to say..." Valerie started.

"We know. You didn't have to say anything. Your energy gave it away that you need some help," replied the green-haired woman. "My name is Liliana, and this is Lagertha," Liliana said as she pointed to the black-haired woman.

"You mean like the Magic the Gathering card and a notorious shield-maiden?" Valerie mocked.

"Something like that. We choose our own names we feel called to after we enter the Craft," Lagertha chimed in.

"Craft? What are you talking about? Look, I really have to go I'm late for class..." Valerie tried to escape out of the booth, but Liliana blocked her path.

"We'll be quick, don't worry. We can sense you're tired of being bullied; looked down on your whole life, right? Can never do anything correctly? Picked on and treated like shit?" Liliana stared deep into Valerie's eyes. Valerie didn't know what was happening, but she suddenly felt she was understood, and a wave of calm rushed over her as she listened to Liliana's soft, creamy voice.

"Yes, but how did you know?"

"Oh, we know everything, sweet," Lagertha said, stealing a piece of pizza out of the box. "We can help you overcome that, you know."

"Please, I really..." Valerie started to say, but stopped and looked at Lagertha. "You can? You mean really get people to stop bothering me and treating me like I'm nothing?"

"Sure. It's easy," Liliana said. "Look, you know Cemetery Hill looking over the campus, right?"

"Yeah, but I've never been there before."

"Just come up the dirt road from the bottom of the hill, there's gates blocking the path, but they'll be unlocked. Meet us tonight around twilight and we'll explain everything. We promise." Liliana scooted out of the booth. She gestured toward the door. "You don't want to be late for class."

"We'll see you tonight," Lagertha mumbled, munching on her stolen pizza.

Valerie nodded, grabbed her bag, and walked out the door, completely forgetting the pizza box on the table. She looked through the window toward Liliana and Lagertha; they were looking back at her and smiling. Valerie could've sworn their eyes were glowing.

2: Cauldron of Changes...We Are the New People

Valerie was of course late to class, again, and Cordelia rolled her eyes as she strolled into labs fifteen minutes late. Cordelia was setting up to test rocks and gemstones of their physical properties after learning about the geological tests in class the day before. Valerie quietly slipped in before Professor Krieger noticed her.

"Where...the *fuck*... have you been?" Cordelia hissed.

"I got held up at Rizzo's. Tony was taking forever to get me a pizza box." Valerie dropped her bag and got out her notes.

"I don't see a damn box in your hands. Where's the pizza?"

"Oh...um..." After what Cordelia said earlier about Liliana and Lagertha, she was afraid to tell her she talked to them. But Cordelia was going to find out sooner or later.

"Those two girls came over and cornered me in the booth. They wanted to talk to me."

Cordelia dropped the rock she had in her hands that she just pulled out of the box. "They did *what?*"

Professor Kreiger looked over at Valerie and Cordelia after hearing the loud clink of the rock on the Formica table, then went back to speaking with his aide.

Valerie gulped. "It wasn't a big deal. They were very nice. Even invited me to meet them later."

"Excuse you, but you're not going to, right? I *told* you to stay away from them! You heard what everyone's been saying!"

"Oh... noooo... no, I was just entertaining them. I'm not really going," Valerie said as she prepared the acidity solution.

"Good. You're actually making a right choice for once."

Valerie rolled her eyes as they began testing the properties of sulfur. She had no intention of telling Cordelia she was going to go.

"Can we get back to the mineral test please?" Valerie huffed.

"Fine."

Except for writing down calculations and test results, the two were quiet for the rest of the lab since Professor Kreiger decided to help them with their tests after Cordelia started gagging on the smell of the acid hitting the sulfur.

That night after classes, Cordelia had to go to her nighttime choir rehearsal, so Valerie was free to sneak up to Cemetery Hill. As she looked in the mirror in her bathroom as she was getting ready, tears started welling up in her eyes. She never saw herself as beautiful with large glasses, bushy brown hair, not-so-straight teeth, and she never wore anything "sexy." She preferred to wear sweatpants and a t-shirt, and sometimes she'd pull out a dress during the summer.

Tonight, the air was chilly, so she opted for a pair of Victoria Secret boyfriend sweats, a Fruits Basket t-shirt, and a zip-up hoodie she got when she went to see Hamilton on Broadway. No wonder people made fun of her; she could never dress appropriately. She wasn't one to wear leggings, a North Face jacket, and Ugg boots. Cemetery Hill wasn't a far walk from her dorm, but her calves still ached from walking halfway across campus to reach the old iron gate and then hoof it uphill on the steep dirt path. As Valerie felt the leaves crunch under her feet, she took in the scent of fall with earthly pinecones and frosted grass. The moon started to rise as the sun set in front of her, changing the sky from its bright blue earlier in the day to hues of plum purple and autumn reds and oranges. Off in the distance, she saw the clouds rolling out from the thunderstorm earlier in the day.

Huh, she chuckled, *what a metaphor for my old life moving out and the new one coming in. At least, I hope so.*

As she reached the hillcrest, an old Victorian building stood at the top with a wrap-around porch and a plethora of windows with flicking candlelight behind the ancient panes. As she started as the fire the flames were dancing, enticing her to come inside. Valerie took a deep breath and tried to calm her heart from pounding out of her chest. She felt an odd sense of calm but was also scared out of her mind at what might happen. Cordelia's voice was in the back of her head. Were they going to use her as a human sacrifice? Turn her into a frog? Hypnotize her to do their dirty work? *Oh stop it,* she thought. *Those myths Cor told you are getting to your head.* She started to walk up the small stone path leading from the road to the door, passing an old gas-lit pole with a lantern at the edge of the road, when the door slowly started to creep open. Lagertha poked her head out from behind the door.

"We knew you'd come. See I told you she'd come, Lil!" She bounced happily from foot to foot.

"Shut up, Lag. Let her in." Valerie heard the other voice announce from behind the door.

Lagertha swung the door open and gestured Valerie to come inside, so Valerie walked up the wooden steps and into the foyer.

She thought this would be an old decrepit, creepy house like something out of Scooby-Doo, but it was actually clean and well-kept like it was just built in the 1800s. She looked up and saw a massive chandelier, complete with real candles, lighting the hall. Everywhere she looked, she didn't see any sort of electricity. As if Lagertha knew what she was thinking, she piped up, "Oh, we do have actual electricity here, but tonight is a special night and called for the Old Ways."

Old Ways...?

As they walked together into the main parlour, Lagertha's bare feet didn't make a sound, while Valerie's soft canvas shoes make a couple of squeaks across the floor. Liliana was sitting in a plush velvet chair near a roaring fireplace. She smiled as Lagertha and Valerie walked into the room.

"Valerie, I feel we owe you an explanation. Sorry for being so cryptic earlier, but we can't speak much of what we do in public. Almost everything you've heard about us is true. We know people whisper rumors about us being witches that practice witchcraft. That's perfectly true." Liliana took a sip of a dark wine-colored drink on the table next to her and waited for Valerie to speak. All Valerie could do was stare, trying to process what Liliana was saying.

"We use magick to help ourselves and others, regardless of what others think." Liliana continued. "After all, we were put here by the gods for a reason. They gave us the ability to manipulate our fate, so why not use it?" Liliana stood up and gestured toward a bookcase. "This bookcase leads to a secret room. If you're ready to learn about how to change your life using magick, you can follow us."

Liliana and Lagertha both approached the bookcase and pulled on a large sconce next to it, both completely in sync. The bookcase slowly creaked open to reveal carpeted steps leading up to the next floor. Liliana walked up the staircase, and Lagertha stood by the door, but Valerie stood frozen. *They really are witches,* she thought. She had come face to face with a Coven and for some reason they wanted her to be a part of it, or sort of asked her if she wanted to be a part of it. *But why?* Valerie couldn't decide if she was going to leave or walk up those stairs.

She was a complete fuck up, after all; why would anyone want her?

Why were they trying to help?

Valerie could hear Cordelia in her head. Valerie already lied to her best friend about going to Cemetery Hill. Could she keep a lie about joining a Coven? But the ability to manipulate her fate... no more of Cole picking on her and treating her like dirt in front of his friends. No more professors humiliating her in class. No more of anyone looking down on her. Valerie smiled a sly smile and headed toward the stairsteps. Lagertha smiled as she saw Valerie approach the steps, start to ascend them, then followed behind her closing the bookcase door behind them. As Valerie walked up the steps, she heard low chanting, almost a whisper. She could hear the crackling of a fire and saw a soft glow coming from the landing above. She could smell incense, the heady scent of patchouli, and something that resembled an earthy stroll in the woods. Valerie could see the whisps of the smoke spilling over the landing. As she reached the top, she found herself at the top of the house, inside a large room with windows overlooking the hill. From here she could almost see the entire city; the lights were just starting to glow in buildings from the coming dark of night.

"I'm glad you deiced to join us," Liliana announced from the center of the room. Around her were other women, about four of them, Lagertha and Valerie made five and six, dressed in robes of different colors from purple to blood red, sparkling gold, and deep blue. The robes had different symbols on them from Norse runes to Egyptian hieroglyphs. Liliana herself was wearing a robe with symbols Valerie couldn't describe.

"What's the meaning behind the robes?" Valerie asked.

"Direct and ready to learn. I like it," Liliana said with a smile. "The robes are each witch's favorite color, which is also their aura color, and the symbols stand for the gods they call upon the most. Lagertha, given her chosen name of course, calls on the Norse gods. Tiye, here," she motioned to a woman in dark green, "calls upon the Egyptian gods. I call upon many different gods, but mainly Mandaean and Greek. Soon you will learn what gods and goddesses are called to you and develop your own robe." Liliana strolled, almost as if she was floating, toward Valerie as she talked. Valerie soaked in the information like a sponge, her mouth started to gape open yearning to learn more.

The women stood in a circle around a large pentagram in the center of the floor. There were runes and symbols around the pentagram. The room was filled with incense, candles, crystals, and each witch carried a ceremonial knife in their belt. A cauldron sat off to the side of the room, and high shelves lined the walls filled with bottles and spell books. In the left corner toward the campus grounds by the courtyard in the south stood a large table covered in a cloth with a large tree and winding branches and a three-moon symbol with two crescent moons on the side of a full moon. It was almost like she was standing in a modern version of Hocus Pocus.

"My best friend Cordelia didn't want me to come. I don't know if I can not tell her I'm becoming a witch," Valerie admitted, her voice slightly wavering and looking toward the ground.

"Don't you worry about that," said Lagertha. "We have ways to keep our Coven a secret."

Tiye turned toward Valerie. "You come stand next to me, honey. You have a family now and you'll never have to worry about being hurt again."

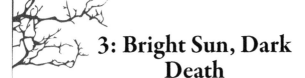

3: Bright Sun, Dark Death

It was the middle of the semester already, and it was All Hallows Eve. Valerie had just ended a Facetime call with Cordelia in the hospital. Tears came to her eyes as she heard Cordelia's once bright and bubbly voice with her quirky manners deteriorated into a croak, with coughing and heavy breathing in between. Seeing her getting better instead of lying in a coma with a ventilator like a few weeks before eased Valerie's mind. She wasn't sure if the Coven had anything to do with it, but she was sure they were responsible for Cor contracting COVID leaving her in the hospital for over a month.

This turn of events left Valerie free to attend meetings at the house on Cemetery Hill. She was busy brushing her hair in the mirror getting ready for a meeting with the girls. She had learned so much from them over the past few weeks, and tonight they were going over the plan for her formal initiation tomorrow night.

As she looked at herself in the mirror, she couldn't believe how much she changed. She now had long, silky, wavy hair with bouncing curls blending from black and bleeding into a wine and violet hue. She started wearing contacts and ditched the chunky glasses, the contacts changed her eyes to a lilac purple. She looked down at her slinky black dress that accentuated her breasts and clung tight to her small waist and hourglass hips. She looked nothing short of a gothic beauty rivaling Morticia Addams. She grabbed her purse and walked out the door after applying some dark purple lipstick and a swipe of eyeshadow.

Now when she was walking out of the dorm and across the campus, she got all the looks in the world. Even Cole started to notice her and hit on her once or twice. He was going to be in for a surprise since the girls told her he was part of her initiation... whatever that meant. As she walked toward Cemetery Hill, she saw her friends Kelly and Jake sitting by the fountain and did her best to walk behind them so they wouldn't see her. That was all she needed was for them to blab to Cordelia. She strolled toward the iron gate and up the hill toward the house. Before she was hesitant to even enter the gate, but now she walked up the road and into the house with a confident air like she lived there.

Liliana was sitting on the porch swing reading Shakespeare's Scottish play. "I see your confidence lessons have helped immensely."

Valerie chuckled. "They have. How fitting what you're reading today. Are we planning a usurp of the throne?"

"Not my throne of course, think of it as the throne of your past."

Valerie and Liliana walked into the house and toward the bookcase. The bookcase was already open, so they padded up the stairs. When they reached the landing, plush chairs were in a circle around the table that was moved into the center of the room. Blazing black candles rested on the centerpiece decorated with pumpkins, acorns, and little pentagrams. Lagertha, Tiye, and the others were already seated around the table. Two chairs were empty, one at each end of the table. Liliana gestured to Valerie to sit down before she made her way around the table to take her seat.

"Val...the time has come for you to formally enter your sisterhood. Tomorrow night you will be a part of this Coven for life. You will keep our secrets of the Craft and use your powers for the greater good of yourself and the group. Do you understand?" Liliana crossed her hands over the table as she spoke.

"Yes, I understand," Valerie breathed.

"In order to become a member of the magickal community, we all have made sacrifices. It is your turn to make this sacrifice and join us," Lagertha announced haughtily.

"Sacrifice?" Valerie's voice rose an octave and a confused look crossed her face. "What am I supposed to give up?"

"It's not what you're giving up, dear." Tiye said in her thick Southern accent. "It's what you're willing to... remove. Permanently."

"Valerie, if you haven't noticed, we don't dabble in white magick. We're dark witches and only do Black magick," Liliana added sternly. "If you wish to not join us, you may. But there will be consequences if you say anything."

Valerie sat speechless. Black magick? Couldn't she get hurt? Something could go wrong and harm her, or them. But she trusted her sisters. She was too deep in now, and she didn't want to turn back. She loved the attention, the way she looked, and the power she had. Since meeting the Coven, somehow she developed the ability to manipulate anything into the way she wanted it.

"No...no it's all right," Valeria said finally. "What do I have to do?"

"I think you'll figure it out." Liliana pulled out an ornate black box with an etched pentagram on it colored a deep red. A gold leaf trim covered the edges of the box. She handed the box to Lagertha who handed the box down one by one to each woman, until Tiye handed it to Valerie. Valerie opened the box to reveal a shining silver knife, complete with etched symbols of Norse runes, a pentagram, and Latin words she couldn't understand.

"'*Requiescat in pace*?'" Valerie read. She looked up at Liliana. "What does that mean?"

"It's the Latin form of *rest in peace*. Use it only on someone who deserves it," Liliana whispered.

Valerie placed the knife back into the box and closed it. She was starting to understand what she was supposed to do. But who was worthy enough of this occasion? Then it dawned on her. It wasn't her childhood bullies she was to use it on, she heard a voice whisper in her head: *Cole.*

Valerie nodded and tucked the box into her large purse.

"Do you mind if I go, guys? I need to prepare for tomorrow."

"No problem." Liliana smiled. "Meet us back here at the witching hour tomorrow, after the job is done."

Valerie picked up her purse, said goodnight to the women, and walked down the stairs to the door.

The entire way down the hill and back to her dorm, her mind was racing.

Kill Cole Dermott.

Kill Cole Dermott?

How in the world was she going to get away with killing one of the most popular, but the biggest asshole narcissistic, chauvinistic pig on campus? And his family was very popular; it wasn't like he was a nobody in town that no one would miss.

How would she make him disappear without a trace?

She felt something stirring in her stomach, something she never felt before. A hot rush washed over her, and suddenly, her doubts left her mind.

The gods would take care of everything.

Back in her dorm room, she looked out of the window toward the crescent moon. It was waning; the perfect time to get rid of someone on Halloween. She watched as everyone was hauling in costumes and spider webbing from their cars, and she could see the gym getting ready for the big Halloween Terror Bash the next day.

The night was almost too perfect.

The air was crisp, but warm enough for a light coat. There wasn't a cloud in the sky and the stars lit up the ground with the moon. Carved pumpkins and hay bales lined the walkways of campus. She wanted to go to bed, but electricity and adrenaline rushed through her body. She felt as if someone was taking control of her. She tried to control her racing heartbeat with deep yoga breaths, but it raced faster and faster. Memories raced through her mind. At six years old, she remembered when Courtney Anderson pulled her hair and pushed her into the mud on the playground. At ten, she remembered when Raqel and her friend jumped her and Brittany on the walk home from the park, breaking her glasses and bloodying her nose so badly her mother called the cops. At fifteen, she remembered when her first boyfriend took advantage of her. When she was sixteen, it came flooding back when that same boyfriend she was terrified to leave held a knife to her stomach and pushed her down the stairs.

The years kept coming back, and wracking sobs sent her body in spasms. The pain, the beatings, the ridicule, the emotional abuse of her parents saying she'd never amount to anything and would be a nobody her entire life.

Then she remembered when she first met Cole. In high school, he tried to molest her by cornering her in the staircase after school. She remembered when he "accidentally" hit her in the head during football practice with the football, and then at the Homecoming game he stole all of her clothes while changing on the bus, so she was forced to get off of the bus in her bra and panties and search for her band uniform and sweats.

The heat and anger rose in her body.

She endured years of abuse from him and so many others, and that was about to end. Her emotions took over, feeling like her body was on autopilot controlled by someone else.

She wasn't waiting until tomorrow night; it was happening now.

She grabbed the box out of her purse and yanked out the knife. In her dresser was a black garter belt. She opened the drawer, grabbed the garter, and quickly pulled it on up her thigh. She stuck the knife inside the belt and pulled her dress back down. Cole's dorm room was on the other side of the building, two floors up. She grabbed her purse and headed to the elevator.

Luckily, she didn't have to go far. After she pressed the up button on the elevator, the doors opened to reveal Cole standing in the corner, wearing his usual plaid unbuttoned shirt and jeans with his cowboy boots.

Oh, this is perfect, she thought. She slunk into the elevator and saw the main floor button was already pressed.

"Hey, Cole. Going down too?" she said huskily.

"Yeah." He eyed her up and down. "Hey Val, you look good tonight."

"Oh, I do? Good, because I was hoping to run into you," she said, inching closer.

"Really? Do tell why, baby." Cole started to reach for her. She allowed him to wrap an arm around her waist.

"Well, I wanted to see if you wanted to walk me over to Rizzo's. The bar upstairs has a Halloween party tonight and I wanted to have a few drinks... maybe do something else by ourselves in the woods behind the building..." She pushed her breasts up against him, leaned in close, and moved his hand down to her ass.

"You're speaking my language," Cole moaned. "C'mon let's go, sexy."

Valerie smiled seductively as the door to the elevator opened. When he walked in front of her to exit, her seductive smile turned to an evil grin. As they walked out of the dorm and up the wooded path to Rizzo's Bar and Pizza, a voice whispered in Valerie's ear again.

Do it now...

Valerie placed a hand around Cole's arm. "Hey Cole..."

"Yeah, toots?"

Before he could say anything else, she grabbed him and kissed him.

"Oh please, Cole I can't wait I *need* you. Can we do it now?"

"Hell, yeah! C'mon you little slut—there's a gazebo over on the off path through the woods."

Cole dragged her off the wooden plank path to a beaten dirt path leading away from campus. A few feet away the gazebo stood with purple and orange lights hanging from the roof. There were paper bats and pumpkins decorating the inside. Cole immediately pushed her onto the bench, grabbing her hair and ramming his lips into hers. She responded, getting him to push his clothed throbbing bulge against her, moving his hands to cover her breasts. He reached in and freed them from her dress, grabbing a handful, squeezing, sucking, and biting the nipples while she moaned in artificial pleasure.

"Please, Cole, please... take me," She moaned.

That was enough for him to hear, and he started to unzip his pants. He entered her quickly, and as he pumped inside her it sounded just like his laughter: a dying pig.

She moaned along with him, trying to keep his interest. When she felt him starting to get close, he started to moan louder. She quickly pulled him in as deep as she could, held him inside her, then pulled out the knife and stabbed him in the back. The knife slid through his flesh like butter. She felt his hot sticky blood pour over her fingers as he screamed in pain. Nobody would know the difference if they heard him as his sounds weren't any different from his orgasms or his laughter.

She yanked the knife out and plunged it between his ribs again.

She smiled as she saw the look on his face, his eyes wide with shock. Blood poured out of his mouth. Valerie quickly pushed him off her and he fell on his back, convulsing from the blood leaving his body.

"You've paid your price for what you've done to me, Cole! And my name isn't Val...it's Kore!" She plunged the knife into his heart this time. Her lips released a wicked laugh as she watched his soul die in his eyes. Valerie heard footsteps in the woods behind her, but she stayed still, staring at his body, his blood soaking the hem of her dress.

"Well done, Kore." Liliana said, coming out of the shadows. Behind her were Lagertha and Tiye. "Nice name to choose, too. The Greek goddess of Death?"

"You were right. I think I've found my gods." Valerie smiled. Liliana grinned and turned toward Lagertha, nodding her head to come forward. Lagertha approached Liliana and Valerie, holding a velvet, black robe.

"You have a little of all of us in you, Kore. You're one of us now," she said as she handed Valerie the robe.

The robe was soft, with a large pentacle in the middle and Nose runes, Greek symbols, and Egyptian hieroglyphs surrounding it, all representing the bringer of death and sexual aggression.

"The sex was a nice touch," Lagertha said, lighting up a cigarette peering briefly at Cole's body.

"I thought so. Hades seemed to think so, too," Valerie said as she gently wiped the blade off on her dress and tasted his blood on her fingers. "You here to help me clean up?"

"What are sisters for?" Tiye replied.

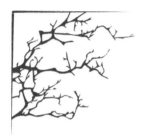

The end

Ashley Brion © 2021

Ashley Brion © 2021

Don't miss out!

Visit the website below and you can sign up to receive emails whenever Ashley Brion publishes a new book. There's no charge and no obligation.

https://books2read.com/r/B-A-CVQP-KZMYB

BOOKS 2 READ

Connecting independent readers to independent writers.

Did you love *Birth of the Wicked*? Then you should read *Illusion at Midnight*[1] by Ashley Bríon!

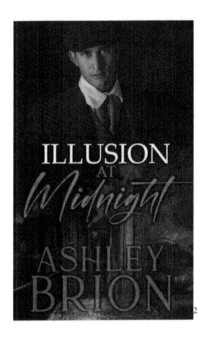

[2]

After spending centuries searching for his lost love, Andre finds her on her last reincarnation as Lily Cordova.

Lily, a witch, has long awaited his arrival but is unprepared for the decision he brings her. As a vampire, he cannot die and follow her into the afterlife once this lifecycle takes her from him. Andre must woo Lily and reignite the memories from her past lives in hopes she will finally choose him.

---

1. https://books2read.com/u/mKdXnd

2. https://books2read.com/u/mKdXnd

As the hurricane barrels their way, Lily has a choice to make: let it sweep her away, leaving her in the afterlife forever, or let Andre turn her into a vampire.

"Though short, this novel is an emotional rollercoaster that will leave readers satisfied and hopeful. Ashley Brion's writing is truly unparalleled." -Robin Ginther-Venneri, owner of Robin's Reviews and KIPS Publishing

Read more at https://www.slucas0.wixsite.com/authorashleybrion.

About the Author

Ashley Bríon is a 2013, 2015, and 2019 BA, MA, and MFA graduate in English and Creative Writing. Ashley has a long history of French and English heritage. She is bilingual speaking both French and English. She spends her free time gaming with her friends, acting, tap dancing, practicing yoga, and playing with her pets. Ashley embraces her love of history and different cultures through her writings, and is autistic and is a "social justice warrior" advocating for LGBTQIA+ and POC rights. Her favorite holidays are Halloween and Christmas and enjoys a cup of sake every evening.

Follow her on all her socials and sign up for her monthly newsletter on her website.

TikTok: @Jokergurl09

Facebook:

www.facebook.com/authorashleybrion

Instagram:

www.instagram.com/Jokergurl_cosplay_ashley_brion

Bookbub:

https://www.bookbub.com/authors/ashley-brion

Read more at https://www.slucas0.wixsite.com/authorashleybrion.

Printed in Great Britain
by Amazon